MIND READER: BLACKMAIL

Pete Johnson has been a film extra, a film critic for Radio 1, an English teacher and a journalist. However, his dream was always to be a writer. At the age of ten he wrote a fan letter to Dodie Smith, author of *The Hundred and One Dalmatians*, and they communicated for many years. Dodie Smith was the first person to encourage him to be a writer.

He has written many books for children as well as plays for the theatre and Radio 4, and is a popular visitor to schools and libraries.

Another book by Pete Johnson

MIND READER

SURFERS

Mind Reader
BLACKMAIL

Pete Johnson

Illustrated by
Ron Tiner

PUFFIN BOOKS

PUFFIN BOOKS

Published by the Penguin Group
Penguin Books Ltd, 27 Wrights Lane, London W8 5TZ, England
Penguin Putnam Inc., 375 Hudson Street, New York, New York 10014, USA
Penguin Books Australia Ltd, Ringwood, Victoria, Australia
Penguin Books Canada Ltd, 10 Alcorn Avenue, Toronto, Ontario, Canada M4V 3B2
Penguin Books (NZ) Ltd, Private Bag 102902, NSMC, Auckland, New Zealand

On the World Wide Web at: www.penguin.com

Penguin Books Ltd, Registered Offices: Harmondsworth, Middlesex, England

First published 1999
1 3 5 7 9 10 8 6 4 2

Typeset in 15/22 Bembo

Printed in England by Clays Ltd, St Ives plc

British Library Cataloguing in Publication Data
A CIP catalogue record for this book is available from the British Library

ISBN 0-141-30291-7

Contents

Chapter One

Losing the Crystal

IT'S ME, MATT again. Up to a few weeks ago I was just an ordinary boy. Now I have a strange, eerie power. Maybe you've read about it, and how my whole life changed because of a crystal.

The crystal belonged to Mrs

Jameson, an old lady I came to know very well. She always wore this crystal round her neck. It fascinated me, perhaps because there were flashes of so many colours in it.

After she died Mrs Jameson left the crystal to me – with a mysterious note. She said no one else must ever discover just how special the crystal was: only me.

It took me a while to discover the crystal's secret, but what a secret. It can read minds.

How does it work? Let me give you a quick demo. Just say you walk past me and I want to know what you're thinking. All I do is move the crystal slightly in your direction, wait a few seconds for it to warm up, then I can hear your every thought, just as if you were whispering them right in my ear.

I can go on ear-wigging until the crystal gets too hot to hold. Then I let it cool down before I start again.

And it doesn't matter how far away you are from me. So you could be up one end of a field and I could be at the other. I can still listen in – or "tune in" as I call it – to you.

By the way, if you're sitting in your house you're still not safe from me. The crystal can eavesdrop through glass too, though not through walls.

Does this sound a bit weird, a bit spooky? I suppose it does. But it's also totally brilliant, isn't it?

I've made some great discoveries. But the crystal has also caused me a fair amount of hassle, especially with Cally, my best mate. After which I made a rule never to use the crystal on my family or good friends again.

I thought I'd learnt all I needed to know about my crystal. But I hadn't. And lately some incredible things have happened which I'd really like to tell you about.

It all started when I did something deeply shaming: I lost my crystal. How could I have been so careless? And with something so precious too. It happened the night of Craig's party. Some of you have met Craig before. If you haven't, I'll describe him to you in three words: sad, slimy, rich.

So why was I going to his party? Good question. But everyone else was going and I suppose I didn't want to miss out. Even though I knew it would depress me to see exactly how big Craig's house was and how much money was wasted on him.

Still, the party was OK-ish: lots of food anyhow. Craig, of course, was just bursting with smugness and spent the whole time showing off. So, actually, did his parents.

His mum was wearing these trendy leather pants and platform shoes. She even had an earring in her nose. I saw Cally staring at her and, just for a laugh, I broke my rule of not tuning in to friends. And Cally was thinking: "She's too old and wrinkly to be wearing an earring in her nose. She just looks ridiculous."

I turned to Cally. "Craig's mum is too old and wrinkly to be wearing an earring in her nose. She just looks ridiculous."

Cally gave a little gasp on hearing me repeat her thoughts but then she quickly said: "Oh, you're so cruel, Matt, she looks all right." I just grinned to myself.

Later we played "Murder in the Dark". Of course there were masses of places to hide. I hid under the stairs. I knew someone was nearby. I could hear him wheezing softly. It sounded exactly like Craig. I decided to check, and reached out for my crystal. I always keep it on my belt. Only it wasn't there.

Well, I was frantic. I forgot all about the game. I searched everywhere for it. Cally joined in too. Finally, she said: "Don't worry, I'll buy you another crystal when I get my birthday money."

How could I tell her the crystal was irreplaceable, priceless?

Craig pretended to hunt for it too. "I'm sure it will turn up, Spud." (That's my nickname because my nose looks a bit like a potato. Hardly anyone calls me that now, except Craig.) But I had the strangest feeling Craig knew more than he was letting on.

Craig doesn't really like me much. (He does like Cally, but that's another story.) So he'd enjoy hiding my crystal and then seeing me sweat as I searched everywhere for it.

Some of us were sleeping over. Cally was sharing a room with two other girls and I was sharing with a boy called Mark.

Mark fell asleep almost at once. The bedroom was very hot: Craig's family could obviously afford to leave the heating on all night. Normally I'd have drifted off to sleep too. But that night I tossed and turned. Where was my crystal?

I was more certain than ever that Craig knew where it was. His room was next to mine. Should I just barge in there and interrogate him?

Suddenly I heard a cry which made me shoot up in bed.

It was Craig – and he was calling for help.

Chapter Two

The Whispering Ghost

NORMALLY I WOULDN'T have lifted a fingernail to help Craig. But there was something about that cry. It sounded desperate. And I seemed to have been the only one who'd heard him. Mark was still sleeping peacefully.

I scrambled out of bed and crept next door.

Craig was standing right by the door. He made me jump. Then I was nearly sick. He was wearing disgusting bright red pyjamas which had his initials on the top pocket.

"What's the matter with you?" I asked.

He didn't answer. He looked as if he'd been turned to stone.

Something weird was going on here.

Then, for the first time, he seemed to notice me. He put his face right up to mine. It was covered in sweat. "I've just heard a ghost."

I'd have laughed except he looked so pale, and he was shaking.

"It was here in my bedroom," he went on. "I heard it whispering at me."

"Whispering," I repeated. Straight away I thought of my crystal. But how could it be mixed up in this? Unless Craig had fallen asleep holding it.

Then Craig's parents rushed in. They were both in their initialled bright red pyjamas too. The three of them looked as if they'd just escaped from the *Starship Enterprise*.

"We thought we heard you cry out," gushed his mum. They perched either side of him on the bed.

Craig told them about the ghostly whispering, while I prowled around his bedroom searching for my crystal. Then his parents, oozing concern, took Craig downstairs for "a sugary drink to calm him down".

I was convinced my crystal was in this room somewhere. I had to find it.

Then, out of nowhere, a voice whispered loudly: "I'm not going to hang around. That wind's got a real sting of winter in it."

It was like someone whispering through a loud-hailer at me. But the room was empty. I drew back the thick curtains. A man in a heavy dark coat was walking vigorously down the road. Was it his thoughts I'd just heard? But how? The crystal only worked when someone was holding it, didn't it?

I glanced down, and there was my crystal, wedged behind the radiator. My heart beat excitedly.

So Craig had found the crystal, just as I'd suspected, and hidden it behind his radiator. That was a really mean thing to do, even for him.

I bent down to grab it, then nearly dropped it again. The crystal was scorching hot. I touched the radiator. That was boiling too.

Suddenly, I had an idea. The crystal must have caught the heat from the radiator. Then as it got hotter it started picking up thoughts through the window. The hotter it got, the louder it got: beaming thoughts into Craig's bedroom in full stereosonic sound. No wonder he was so terrified.

I heard footsteps coming up the stairs. I was about to rush out with my crystal but then I decided to teach Craig a lesson. I nearly laughed out loud at my idea. Still, Craig deserved it.

I hastily returned the crystal to its place behind the radiator, exactly as I'd found it, tilted slightly towards the window.

I crept back to my room. I waited for Craig's parents to leave. They were ages. I heard them reassure Craig he wouldn't have any more bad dreams. I grinned to myself. That's what they thought. At last they returned to their own room.

I started to get dressed. Suddenly I stopped. I didn't need to go outside, did I? I could just . . .

I opened the window and stuck my head out as far as it would go. Would the crystal pick up my thoughts? I was about to find out. So was Craig.

But I was interrupted by a sleepy voice demanding: "What on earth are you doing?"

I turned round. "Hi, Mark, just getting a breath of fresh air."

"But it's the middle of the night – and it's freezing."

"Shan't be long. I'm just clearing my sinuses."

I pushed my head out again. Then I thought: "Tonight, Craig, you stole something, a crystal, which belongs to Matthew. That was very wrong of you. I am Matthew's guardian angel and I will send ghostly people to haunt you for ever unless you return it to its rightful owner. But hurry up, Craig, you haven't got long." For good measure I added, "Your parents can't save you this time . . . Beware . . . Beware."

"Haven't you finished yet?" Mark was sitting up in bed, staring at me.

"Yeah, my sinuses are completely fine now, thanks."

I closed the window. I'd just got back into bed when I heard footsteps.

"Pretend to be asleep," I hissed at Mark.

"What's going on now?" he muttered, but he did as I'd asked.

The bedroom door opened. It was Craig. He crept towards me. I heard a tiny chink as he placed something on the little cabinet by my bed.

I half-opened my eyes. It was my crystal. Its colours shone in the darkness. Craig tiptoed out again, closing the bedroom door quietly behind him.

Mark asked: "What did Craig just do?"

"I think he found my crystal for me."

"Funny time to bring it back."

"Craig's a funny guy. Still, better late than never. 'Night."

I looked down at the crystal nestling in my hand. I was determined I'd never lose it again.

Chapter Three

In Trouble

THE FOLLOWING NIGHT when everyone in my house was asleep I wrote up what had happened. I have a special exercise book, entitled THE THIRD EAR (the code-name for the crystal).

This is what I wrote.

AMAZING DISCOVERY: The third ear works when put behind a radiator and allowed to get hot. As it gets hotter the whispering becomes much louder.

IMPORTANT: When you hold the third ear only you can pick up the thoughts. But if it is behind a boiling hot radiator, anyone in the room can "overhear" what is being thought.

More soon.

I was so excited about all this I did something stupid.

My family don't usually keep the heating on at night. But we were having such a cold snap, my mum decided this once she would leave it on. So I couldn't resist jamming my crystal at the back of the radiator and then waiting to overhear the thoughts of whoever walked past my window.

Only no one at all walked past, and so I fell asleep. Later I jumped awake. At first I thought someone was in my room. In a way someone was. This man was hissing away in the darkness about why he hated his cousin.

To be honest, he scared me out of my wits. And the voice was so loud. I didn't like it at all. I must move the crystal right now. But then a shadow stepped towards me, and became my mum.

"Matthew, what are you doing letting your radio blare out like that?"

Of course, what my mum had heard wasn't anything to do with the radio.

"Sorry, Mum, I just couldn't sleep."

"Do you know what time it is? I've got such a lot to do tomorrow, with your dad away, and all."

"I won't switch it on again, Mum."

She huffed a bit more and turned to go. Then, to my complete horror, a voice hissed: "I'm sick of her going on at me for nothing. She's a real pain these days."

Mum was back in my room in an instant, glaring furiously at me. "What did you just say? How dare you be so rude, Matthew. And I didn't have a go at you about nothing."

"I know. Sorry. It was just a joke."

"A joke?" spluttered my mum.

I was terrified the crystal was going to pick up another passer-by's thoughts: maybe a woman this time. How could I explain that?

Desperate to get rid of Mum, I buried myself down in my bed. "Sorry again, Mum. 'Night," I burbled.

And I tell you, the very second she left I was out of bed, yanking my crystal away from the radiator. Only it was so hot I dropped it on the carpet. I had to scoop it up in a tissue and then leave it on the little table by my bed. I was very angry with myself. I'd been a real banana-brain tonight.

Next morning at breakfast the atmosphere was distinctly chilly. This was a shame, as lately Mum and I had been getting on well. And I was mad keen to have a dog. Mum wasn't. But I'd started to talk her round, and only last night she and I had chatted about adopting a dog from the local Animal Rescue Centre. Some chance now.

At school the first person I saw was Craig, which really cheered me up! I kept noticing him giving me these sly glances. It was as if he were studying me. I became uneasy. Had Craig guessed there was something special about my crystal? Surely not.

Then something happened which wiped all that from my mind. It was Cally's birthday in a couple of weeks. I was planning to get her something to do with Spurs (she is their number one fan). But I wasn't sure what, as she had so much supporters' stuff already. Anyway, I was waiting for her after school. We always wait for each other by the lockers. She came rushing over to me. "Oh my gosh," she said. "You'll never guess what's happened."

"Amaze me."

"Craig's just given me this for an early birthday present." She waved her left hand at me. On it now were two watches: her old one, and a brand new, big, chunky diver's watch, complete with stop-watch button and an alarm. I could hardly bear to look at it.

"That must have cost a few quid," I muttered.

"I wasn't expecting it at all."

"It's a wicked waste of money."

She nodded.

"And I mean, there are some things you just don't do."

"I was really shocked."

"But you're still going to wear it?"

"Well, yes." Her voice fell. "I do need a new watch, and anyway, I don't think he can take it back."

I didn't say much else. I was too

eaten up with jealousy and anger. I could never compete with a present like that. Trust Craig to throw his money about. And I knew why he was throwing his money about too. He wanted to go out with Cally.

We'd always been rivals where she was concerned. Cally and I had been best friends for hundreds of years – well, two, to be precise. For a while now I'd wondered if she and I would one day go out together. I wanted that very badly. But I wasn't sure if . . . well, to be honest, I wasn't sure if Cally liked me enough.

That's what stopped me asking her out. But I couldn't afford to dither any more.

I had to find out.

Or, rather, my crystal would.

Chapter Four
Helping Cally

ON FRIDAY, AFTER school, I decided to discover – with the help of my crystal – what my chances with Cally were.

There was only one place private enough for this. The oak tree in a wood just a stone's throw away from Cally's house.

Cally and I love tree-climbing. But the oak tree was our favourite because it was quite easy to climb: there was even a hole in the trunk where you could lift yourself up. And, best of all, about halfway up, it had a wide comfortable branch that was just right for sitting on. So in the summer Cally and I would sit there for hours, telling spooky stories and talking about things. There was also an epic view, stretching right across our village and the town beyond.

But now it was the beginning of October and Cally looked stunned when I suggested climbing our oak tree.

"Be a bit cold, won't it?" she said.

"We've got coats on."

She smiled. "Oh, why not?"

Climbing up a tree in a coat and scarf is actually quite hard. Our sleeves kept catching on the branches, so we were stopping all the time to disentangle ourselves.

"This is a bit like swimming with your clothes on," cried Cally.

"Can't say I've ever tried that," I replied.

We picked our way to the branch, settled ourselves, then Cally said: "So, what do you want to talk about?"

"Well, nothing really."

"Yes you do. Come on – and hurry up. It's freezing."

Well, I knew I couldn't ask her outright if she liked me. I had to build up to it. So I said: "I just wanted to chat about the cinema."

"The cinema," she echoed.

"Yeah. I just wondered what actors you like these days," I said, with my crystal poised ready.

Now, I know what you're thinking – I'd forgotten my vow not to use the crystal on Cally. Well, I hadn't forgotten my vow, exactly. I'd just decided if the crystal found out she didn't fancy me I'd be saving Cally loads of embarrassment too.

So Cally rattled on about what movie stars she liked. While the crystal heard: "I've got a horrible feeling I know why Matt is asking me these questions. I really hope I'm wrong."

That didn't sound very promising. But I pressed on. "Do you prefer guys with blond hair or dark hair?" (I've got black hair.)

She gabbled something about how

"it depended on the rest of the guy's face". But I was too busy listening to my crystal: "I'm going to pretend I don't know what this is leading up to. But I do. I've always dreaded this moment. Matt's going to ask me out, isn't he?"

There wasn't much point in asking any more questions. I knew the outcome: no sale.

But then I "overheard": "Of course I do think Matt is fit." Immediately a great big smile plastered itself across my face.

"What are you smiling at?" asked Cally.

"Nothing." I started to giggle. Cally thinks I'm fit.

"Come on, tell me," said Cally.

"No, I just feel good, that's all," I said.

But I couldn't get rid of that smile. "You were saying why you don't like boys with blond streaks."

She carried on talking, while the crystal "overheard": "Matt's behaving very oddly tonight. But he mustn't ask me out, because if we go out together and then break up . . . why, we'll end up nowhere. And I'll have lost my best friend. I can't risk that. Besides, tonight couldn't be a worse time . . . not when I'm so worried and upset. I'm surprised Matt hasn't noticed."

"You're worried about something, aren't you, Cally?" I asked.

She started. And for the first time I noticed how pale and washed-out she looked.

"If anyone realized, I knew it would be you," she said. "There's just a terrible atmosphere in my house at the moment." She stared out at the thousands of roofs and aerials below us. "My parents are really upset about something. They keep whispering in corners. Either they're about to get divorced or it's to do with me. I know they're cross about all my low marks at school. So I wouldn't be surprised if they're plotting to send me away to another school."

I sat up. "They mustn't do that."

"I just wish they'd tell me what's wrong. But they won't and it's really doing my head in."

"I'm not surprised."

Right then I decided I'd solve this mystery for Cally: me and my crystal. I felt a bit like those knights in old tales, who, before they can win the hand of the girl, have to perform a daring task.

I performed my daring task on Saturday afternoon. I was sitting inside the kitchen with Cally and her pet dog, Bess. Her dad was out in the garden, vigorously brushing up some of the autumn leaves.

Cally was asking me about the history homework. She was anxious to do it right. I stood by the window, talking to her. But I had my crystal trained on Cally's dad. So it was like trying to listen to two different conversations at once.

Often people don't think in sentences, especially if they're very angry and upset. They just splutter out the odd word. That's exactly what happened with Cally's dad. So it took a while to work out what was bugging him.

But at last I'd sussed it. And I couldn't wait to tell Cally. So later that afternoon when we were taking Bess for a walk I blurted out, "I wonder if your dad's got worries at work. A lot of people do these days, you know. Maybe he's on a shortlist of six, four of whom will lose their jobs because of –" I repeated the word I'd overheard from Cally's dad – "restructuring."

"No, it's not that," said Cally. "My dad's job is totally secure."

"I wouldn't be so sure," I said.

We even had a little argument about it.

Then, the following afternoon, Cally rang and asked to meet up in the wood again. She sounded worked up. I got there early. But Cally was already waiting for me.

"Anything wrong?" I asked.

She smiled. "Let's go tree-climbing again."

It had rained earlier and the branches were wet and slimy and difficult to grip properly. We clambered to our spot.

Then Cally exclaimed: "I can't believe it. You were exactly right. I asked my dad outright if he was worried about losing his job. He looked totally stunned. Then Mum came in and they both told me about this – and it was exactly the word you used – restructuring.

"Dad's certain he's for the chop. He said he and Mum hadn't told me as there was no sense in me worrying as well. If they'd only realized . . ." She smiled at me. "But what I don't get is how you knew. I mean, you were only in our house for about half an hour but you worked it all out."

"Just a lucky guess . . . I guess." I wanted to change the subject now.

"But it's uncanny. I mean, he's on a shortlist of six, and four of them will lose their jobs, exactly as you said."

I realized I'd given Cally too many details. I shifted uneasily. "Lucky guess," I repeated.

Cally wasn't convinced. I could tell. I went on: "And then it happened to this uncle of mine."

"What uncle?"

"Raymond, Uncle Raymond." That was the first name which came into my head.

"I've never heard you mention him."

"No, well, I don't tell you about all my relations. He's not very interesting anyhow. I don't see him much. I just know he was on a shortlist and lost his job."

"Where did he work?"

"Er, Birmingham. In this factory."

"Does he still work there?"

"Yes, he does."

"And you've visited him in Birmingham?" This was turning into an interrogation.

"Once or twice . . . long time ago now." Then I hastily changed the subject. We sat talking about much more important things: like how I could persuade my mum to get a dog.

Grey darkness was rising up like smoke now, blotting out our marvellous view. A sparrow came bombing towards the oak tree, discovered us roosting there, and started flapping like mad before it shot away again.

"Poor thing, discovering us in its house," said Cally.

I was about to reply when suddenly Cally started whispering. I thought for a moment I'd activated the crystal without realizing it. But her lips were moving.

She whispered, confidingly: "You haven't really got an Uncle Raymond in Birmingham, have you?"

She took me completely by surprise. "Yes I have. Well, sort of."

"Sort of." I could see her smiling at me.

"OK, I haven't."

"I can always tell when you're lying, you know."

"Can you?"

"Tell me the truth now. How did you know?"

I shrugged my shoulders. "OK, you tell me."

"All right." She smiled again. "You've made quite a few lucky guesses lately, haven't you?" She leant forward. "Ever since you got that crystal."

Chapter Five

Telling My Secret

THAT GAVE ME quite a shock, I can tell you. Without realizing it, Cally had stumbled on my secret. Of course she was saying it as a kind of joke.

"So can the crystal tell the future?" she asked.

"Maybe," I teased.

"There's something magical about it, isn't there?"

"Very definitely." I was still messing about but not completely. Ever since I'd found out how special my crystal was I'd longed to share the secret with someone, with Cally.

It's a bit like someone giving you a football. Yes, you can play with it on your own – do kick-ups and stuff. But only for so long. After a while you've got to have someone to kick the ball to, haven't you?

That was exactly how I felt about my crystal. It was only half the fun with just me knowing about it. And yes, I'll admit I wanted to impress Cally too.

Of course I remembered what Mrs Jameson had said: how I must keep the secret. But way up here, with Cally, I felt suddenly reckless, and daring.

"Do you really want to know how I found out about your dad?"

"Yes," she cried. The leaves were forming a pattern of shadows over her face. I could hardly see her. It made me feel as if I were talking to her in a dream.

"I've wanted to tell you for so long, Cally."

"Tell me what?" she screamed.

"Do you promise to keep what I tell you a secret?"

"I promise to throw you off this tree if you don't tell me right now."

"OK. I knew what was worrying your dad because I used my crystal to read his mind."

The wind stirred. It set the branches

rattling and shaking. Even the smallest breeze sounds much louder when you're up a tree.

Cally smiled at me. "So you can read minds?"

"With my crystal, I can read anyone's mind – even yours."

"Prove it."

"All right, I will. Think of a number and I'll tell you what number it is."

"Will you? Right, I'm thinking of my number."

"Wait a sec. You've got to let the crystal warm up."

"Oh, it has to warm up, does it? A bit like my nan's old telly."

She was laughing, while I frowned with concentration. "Now, think of your number."

And into my head she whispered:

"What is Matt up to now? He acts so funny sometimes."

"Think of your number," I urged.

The crystal picked up: "This is silly but seven . . . my number's seven."

I stared across at her. "Your number's seven."

A gasp escaped from her lips. But then she said: "Come on Matt, that's an old trick. People always think of seven, don't they?"

I shook my head.

"So how were you able to do that? You've got it out of a book, haven't you?"

I shook my head again.

"And stop shaking your head at me. This has got to be a trick. You can't really read minds with that crystal."

Suddenly the tree shook. The leaves

around us were going like the clappers now. It was almost as if the tree was trying to talk to me, warning me to stop, while Cally still wasn't convinced.

But I couldn't stop now. I held the crystal in my hand again. "Think of a word, any word you like, a word that doesn't exist if you like." I spoke really quickly, like an eager salesman. "Go on."

She gave an uneasy laugh, then half-closed her eyes. At once the word came through to me: "Spuckle."

"Spuckle." I grinned. "What kind of word is that?"

"I know." She smiled, but then her smile vanished into the darkness. "But how were you able to . . ." Her voice fell away. "How exactly did you do that?"

I waved the crystal at her.

"No, no."

And I "overheard": "If this is some kind of joke, Matt's carrying it too far."

"It's not some kind of joke, Cally," I said.

She choked off a cry. She drew back from me. Then, all at once she started to scramble down the tree.

"Cally, where are you going?"

"Why don't you wave your crystal at me and find out," she cried. "No, I'll save you the trouble. I'm getting as far away from you as possible."

Chapter Six

The Crystal's Powers

I WATCHED CALLY with mounting horror. I couldn't let her go like this. What a mess.

"Cally, come back." I started to clamber down after her. She was so worked up I was worried she might fall. But it was me who lost my footing.

The worst thing about falling from a tree is you drop down backwards. So you can't do it in a cool way or make out you meant to do it. And you look so completely undignified people can react in only one way: by laughing loudly.

That's what Cally did.

Suddenly I wasn't scary any more – just ridiculous.

I had to laugh too – until I realized that I had lost my crystal again. It must have slipped off my belt when I fell.

"The crystal's gone," I cried, struggling to my feet.

It was Cally who found it. It had rolled on to a pile of dead leaves.

"Here's your magic crystal," she said.

"Thanks." I carefully put it back on my belt.

She knelt down beside me. "So what am I thinking now?"

I tilted my crystal towards her, and moments later I "overheard": "It's incredible if it's true, but spooky too. The person with that crystal has got so much power."

Then I repeated word for word what she'd been thinking.

She stared at me. "I don't know what to say – or think. It's just incredible."

I nodded, enjoying her wonderment.

"So how long have you had the crystal?"

We went back up the tree and I told her the whole story. She listened, hardly saying anything, only exclaiming at certain events.

When I'd finished she said: "And you haven't told anyone else about your crystal's powers?"

"Only you."

"Only me." She let out a sigh. "Thanks, Matt, and I'm sorry if I . . ."

"Oh, come on, it's a bit of a shocker, isn't it?"

"And it will work on anyone?"

"Oh yes."

She grinned. "Prove it."

We climbed back down and made for the high street. There was hardly anyone about. The first person we saw – of all people – was Craig. He just nodded and waved at us. He was sitting on a wall by himself on the opposite side of the road. I let Cally borrow the crystal. She tapped into him. Afterwards I asked her what Craig had been thinking.

She smiled. "First of all he wondered if we'd noticed his new trainers."

"How pathetic."

"Then he couldn't understand why I was going around with you and not him. Bit sad really."

"Don't go feeling sorry for him," I cried accusingly.

"I'm not."

"The nerve of him thinking that," I muttered.

Next we spotted a well-dressed man with thinning brown hair strolling in front us. Again I let Cally tune into him. He was imagining himself scoring the winning goal at a cup final. Cally kept whispering bits to me.

Then she rushed forward, tapped the man on the shoulder and said: "Brilliant goal."

The man let out a cry and jumped right up in the air, just as if a firework had exploded in his trousers.

"Did you see that?" exclaimed Cally. "Look at him."

The man was now half-running away from us. He kept turning back, gazing at us in fear and amazement.

"He can't believe his ears," cried Cally.

"And are you surprised?" I replied. "You've just read his most private, secret thoughts. Actually, we've got to be careful."

"I know, I know." She shook her head. "This crystal is so incredibly powerful, isn't it?"

We were silent for a moment, then we thought of that man leaping up into the air and we both started to laugh. Soon, tears were falling down our faces and still we couldn't stop.

After that we climbed up the tree

again. It was getting late. We should have both set off home now. But neither of us could stop talking about the crystal.

Then Cally said: "On Friday when you asked me who I liked . . . you used the crystal on me, didn't you?"

I hung my head a little. "Afraid so."

"And you picked up that I thought you were fit?"

Immediately a smile started to form across my face.

"But I was afraid if we went out together it would ruin our friendship."

"Yes," I said quietly.

"Yet, tonight," she said, "you took a chance telling me about the crystal. I think I can take one too. So if you still want to go out with me . . ."

I could only nod.

Happiness took all my words away.

We agreed we wouldn't tell anyone about us yet. People like Craig would make stupid jokes. We'd wait and pick the right moment.

"Will you promise me just one thing?" said Cally. "You won't ever use the crystal on me, because I have horrible thoughts sometimes that aren't true and well . . . I'd never have a private moment."

"I promise," I cried. "And if you ever find out I have used it on you, you can have the crystal."

"What?" she gasped.

"No, I mean it, because then I'll have broken my promise to you and I won't be worthy of the crystal."

I glanced down at the wood below. It was very dark and still and full of shadows . . . and then I saw one of those shadows start to move. It seemed to rise up out of the darkness.

My flesh froze. I thought at first it was Mrs Jameson come to haunt me for breaking my promise, and not keeping the secret.

Then it moved again.

I hissed to Cally: "Someone's down there."

"Listening to us?" Her voice was suddenly hushed.

"Could be." I suddenly realized that we'd both been talking about the crystal at the top of our voices. Someone could be waiting down there, ready to jump us and steal the crystal.

We squinted into the darkness, then Cally cried out: "It's a cat."

Green eyes stared up at us, then

darted away. Cally let out a great sigh of relief. I didn't say anything but I still had a few niggling doubts. What if there had been someone else prowling about there as well as the cat? Someone crouching in the darkness, listening to everything we'd said?

But after a few minutes my doubts started to fade away. It had just been a cat, hadn't it? I noticed again Craig's watch on Cally's arm. And I said: "I wish I had a present to give you to remember tonight."

"Well, I'll tell you what," said Cally. "At my little cousin's tea-party yesterday I got this." She dug in her pocket and produced a gold-looking ring with a white sparkly stone. "I like it, so why don't you give me that?"

"A ring from a cracker?"

"It's the thought that counts." She handed me the ring. Then, feeling a bit silly, I gave the ring back to her. She placed it on her finger.

"One day soon I'll get you a much better one," I said.

"I'll keep this ring for ever," she replied.

I think she meant it.

Next morning I woke up feeling so happy. I was really pleased I'd told Cally about the crystal too. Somehow it had brought us closer together. And I was convinced that shadow I'd seen had only been a cat – until I reached my school.

There, sellotaped to my locker, was an envelope with my name in capitals on the outside. I ripped it open. Inside was a folded-up piece of paper torn from an exercise book. Printed in capitals was a message which chilled my whole body: I KNOW ABOUT THE CRYSTAL.

Chapter Seven
Blackmail

I SHOWED CALLY the note.

She looked horror-struck. "So you were right. Someone was eavesdropping on us."

I nodded gravely.

"Still," she said, "at least we know it was someone from this school."

"I bet I know exactly who wrote that note," I said. "It's got to be Craig."

Cally didn't look so sure.

"We saw him last night, didn't we? I bet he followed us." I frowned.

"Don't say anything yet," said Cally. "We don't want to rattle him, otherwise, well, he could do anything."

For the rest of the day I tailed Craig with my crystal. I didn't pick up anything incriminating at first. But then I "overheard" him thinking about the English test on *Julius Caesar* this Wednesday. He was worrying about it, as the results would go on our report.

Then, after school, a second envelope was stuck to my locker. I tore it open, feeling sick inside even before I'd read it. This one had been written on a computer. It said:

I will keep your secret about the crystal but on one condition. You must tell me what questions will be in the English test on *Julius Caesar* on Wednesday. Leave the questions in the empty locker (number sixty-six) on the bottom left hand side, straight after school tomorrow. Do not wait for me or try and see me.

If you do not follow my instructions I will tell everyone about your crystal. If you obey my instructions I won't bother you again.

I showed the note to Cally. She looked really miserable. "This is all my fault. If you hadn't told me about the crystal, none of this would have happened."

"Don't be silly." I didn't blame Cally at all but I did blame myself. And these mystery notes had taken the shine off last night.

On the way home we talked about what I should do.

"If I find out the questions I'll be giving in to blackmail, and Craig will come back again and again, won't he?"

"He said he wouldn't bother you again."

"Do you believe that?"

"Well, maybe."

I shook my head. "I could wait by the lockers after school and . . ."

"And what?"

"Fight him."

Cally started tut-tutting. "And what good will that do? He'll definitely go off and tell everyone about the crystal then."

Cally was right. I had no choice but to give in to blackmail.

Next day in English I looked around the class. I was pretty certain it was Craig, but I suppose everyone in the class was a suspect. I did a bit of surfing and picked up that other people in the class were worried about the test tomorrow. It didn't really get me any further.

At the end of the lesson everyone rushed off for lunch while I hovered around. Cally whispered, "Good luck," then she left too.

The English teacher, Mrs Stacey, had taught at my school for years. She was a good teacher: helpful, but brisk and no-nonsense. However, for some reason she liked me.

I moved towards her, clutching my crystal.

"Yes, Matt, what can I do for you?"

"I just wanted to ask you about the test tomorrow."

"What about it?"

"Well, I wondered if there'd be a question about the quarrel between Cassius and Brutus."

"Now, Matt, you know I can't tell you that. But you'll be fine tomorrow." She turned her back on me. "Now, off you go."

Mrs Stacey was thinking about a concert she'd be attending tonight, and how she'd do all her preparation in her free period after lunch.

This was dreadful. I wanted Mrs Stacey to be thinking about what was in the test – not her plans for tonight.

I uttered a kind of yelp.

She turned round, alarmed.

"What's wrong, Matt?"

"Nothing, Miss. I just feel a little faint. Is it all right if I sit down a minute?" I gave another little yelp and fell on to a chair.

I had all her attention now. She was leaning over me. I could smell her breath. It reeked of coffee. "Matt, do you want me to get Nurse?"

"No, no," I said hastily. "It's just I've been up late revising *Julius Caesar*."

She looked concerned. "But, Matt, you're a good student. You needn't worry."

"I do, though. I've been up worrying

for hours wondering if there'll be a question on omens and superstitions, or the battles at the end of the play . . ."

She pulled up a chair. She began to talk about *Julius Caesar*, and, more importantly, to think about it. The crystal picked up four of the six questions in tomorrow's test (and we only had to answer three). As I "heard" the questions I realized that I was cheating too. I'd know what was going to be in the test as well.

After I left Mrs Stacey I ran off to the back field and wrote the questions down. At the bottom I added: "I will not do this for you ever again."

Then at the end of school I made for locker sixty-six. It was dented right in the middle and the lock was permanently broken. Inside was a pair of old football boots. They smelt as if they'd been in there since the school was built.

I took them out and cleared the locker of all its antique sweet papers. Then I folded up the question sheet and slipped it inside.

Only Cally knew what I was doing. She gave my hand a squeeze. We walked out of school together.

"I've got to know who's sending me these notes," I said.

"But he said not to wait," cried Cally.

"I won't wait by the school," I said. "But I'll keep watch."

Our school was at the end of a road. Along the road was a bakery and coffee shop. Cally and I could stake out in there, then we'd see anyone returning to school.

"We must be clever," said Cally. "If we do see Craig or someone else from our class we've got to trail them, but they mustn't know we're on to them."

At that moment Craig passed the window. He was on his way back to school. We both ducked down.

"Did he see us?" asked Cally.

"I don't think so."

"Look, I'm going to trail him," I said.

"I think it's best I go after him," said Cally. "I won't get as worked up as you." She got up. "You wait here. I won't be long."

I ordered another coffee. But I couldn't drink it. My insides were turning somersaults.

And then I saw two more girls from my English class half-running towards the school.

I had a sudden, horrible thought: what if more than one person knew about my crystal? Maybe both those girls had written the note.

I had to follow them.

Chapter Eight

Breaking My Promise

THE TWO GIRLS walked quickly into school.

I followed at what I hoped was a safe distance. Craig was still my chief suspect, but anyone from my English group could have written that note.

The two girls were making for the

cloakroom. They walked over to the lockers. My heart was pumping away now.

"Here it is," cried one of the girls. She brought out a copy of *Julius Caesar*.

"Thank goodness I hadn't lost it," she exclaimed. "I knew I'd put it somewhere."

The two girls went off, giggling and chatting together.

A hand touched me on the shoulder. I whirled round.

"I thought I told you to stay in the café?" It was Cally.

"Did Craig take the note?"

"I'm not sure," said Cally. "He went past the lockers all right, but by the time I got near him he was striding off to the science block. I followed him there and saw him talking to one of the teachers about something. Then he went out of the school again."

I marched over to locker sixty-six. "We'll soon know what Craig's been up to."

I opened it up. It was empty.

"The questions have gone," I said softly.

Cally paled. "I'm so sorry, Matt. It's just I didn't want him to spot me, so I kept way back . . ."

"Don't worry, we've got all the evidence we need. It's him."

"We don't know for certain. And even if it was Craig, well, maybe he'll keep his promise."

Suddenly I had an odd feeling of unease. Did Cally know more than she was letting on? After all, Craig had given her that expensive watch. Was she trying to protect him? My fingers twitched around the crystal.

I'd promised Cally I'd never use it on her. But something wasn't right about all this.

We went through Ashton Wood. We were going to chat, up in the oak tree. But on the way, when Cally wasn't looking, I tuned the crystal on to her.

It was then I made a terrible discovery.

Chapter Nine
Message from Mrs Jameson

ONLY ONE THOUGHT was racing through Cally's mind: "If Matt finds out what I've done. If he sees the paper in my pocket . . . or somehow it falls out . . ."

I just looked at her. I was too shocked

to know how to react. Now she was thinking: "I must act calm. That's all I've got to do. Matt would never suspect me. This nightmare will be over soon."

She linked my arm. "Come on, cheer up. I think you might get a pleasant surprise. Craig's got what he wants. I bet he doesn't bother you again."

I gave her a thin smile. Her right pocket was the nearest to me. I pulled out a piece of paper. I recognized my messy handwriting right away. I felt sick. Cally's eyes were huge, while her jaw had dropped down almost to her throat.

"But how . . ." she gasped. Then she saw the crystal. It was still in my other hand. "You promised you'd never use it on me," she snapped.

"Never mind that," I cried. "You

wrote those notes, didn't you, Cally?"

Her mouth set sulkily. "Yes." Then she added quickly, urgently, "Matt, I had no choice. I was desperate to get some good marks. You know how my parents go on and on about my low grades. This was my chance . . ."

"So why didn't you ask me? I probably would have done it." I paused. "Yes, I would have done it – for you. But instead, you went about it in such a shabby way."

"It wasn't meant to be shabby. And I was only going to do it the once. I thought this was the best way. You must believe me."

"You expect me to believe anything you say now?" I paced about. "There I was, thinking how helpful you were following Craig for me. When all the time you were taking the questions for yourself."

"But what harm's been done?"

"What harm?"

Her voice rose shrilly. "Well, if you'd kept your promise to me you'd never have known, and we'd both be much happier now."

I turned away. I couldn't bear to talk to her any more. "I never knew you could stoop to anything so . . ."

"Well, now you do," cried Cally. "And can I have my questions back, please?"

I whirled round. We stared hard at each other.

"All right," I said softly. "You're only cheating yourself." I held the questions out to her.

She snatched them away from me.

She glared at me. "You said if ever you used the crystal on me you'd let me have it because you'd be unworthy of it. Remember?"

For a moment I thought she was going to try and grab my crystal. I immediately leapt back. She laughed mockingly. "Don't worry, I won't take your precious crystal."

She walked away.

I called after her. "Are you going to tell anyone else about . . . about it?"

She didn't answer.

I just stood there. Even in my coat I was shivering. Cally was the one person I trusted. It was the worst moment of my life. I'd never felt more lonely.

Finally, I crawled home.

I tried to revise *Julius Caesar*. But there were too many thoughts swirling around in my head. And every time I thought of Cally, a fresh storm of anger raged in my head. I kept blinking away tears.

Then my mum started fussing about me and being really nice. She hadn't been this nice to me since I had mumps, over two years ago.

Something was odd here. I used the crystal on Mum and eventually discovered that Mrs Stacey had called her, and told Mum she thought I was over-working.

I also picked up that Mum was changing her mind about getting me a dog. She decided I needed something to take my attention off my school-work. Normally I'd have been over the moon. But everything was ruined now.

Next day I dreaded seeing Cally at

school. It would just be so horrible. But in the end, she didn't turn up. She was away ill. So after all that fuss she missed the *Julius Caesar* test.

I only attempted the two questions I hadn't "overheard" yesterday. Every time I stopped and looked up, Mrs Stacey was smiling encouragingly at me. I felt such a fraud.

I kept thinking about Cally. I missed her. But I was still bitterly angry with her too. When she came back I wondered if we'd even be talking. Would she try to blackmail me again? I doubted that, but it was all such a mess.

What should I do now? There was no one I could go to and ask for help. How I wished Mrs Jameson was here now. She'd help me, for sure.

After school I found myself standing outside her house. There was a FOR SALE notice outside it, and the garden, which she'd looked after so carefully, was thick with weeds.

I didn't know what I was doing here. Mrs Jameson wasn't suddenly going to pop up and advise me. Not even the crystal could conjure up Mrs Jameson again.

But I held the crystal in my hand and thought: "Mrs Jameson, I can't believe you're far away from your beloved crystal, even now. I know I should never have told Cally about the crystal but I have done, and what should I do now? Help me, and advise me somehow, please."

Then I went into the local shop just across the road from Mrs Jameson's house. I'd been in there many times before on errands for her, and the old shopkeeper recognized me. We chatted for a bit.

I still had the crystal in my hand. Without me realizing it, the crystal was squeezing itself out of my hand. All at once it fell from my grasp and on to a stack of newspapers tied up with string, on the ground beside me.

I knelt down. It was our local paper. The crystal had landed on the bottom of the page. I picked it up. Underneath the crystal was a small photograph of a woman and a caption:

LOTTERY WIN COST ME ALL MY FRIENDS

Full story page seven.

Without knowing why, I persuaded the shopkeeper to untie the papers so I could buy one. I walked home reading page seven.

This woman had won three million on the lottery. She said the news had changed her friends' attitude to her immediately. Their first thought was, "What's in it for me?" They all came to her with a shopping list of things they wanted.

She was indignant and hurt and felt her friends were just using her. She fell out with them all. But then she said: "I realized something as amazing as a lottery win was bound to set my friends dreaming. Now I want them to contact me . . ."

At home I read the article again and again. I kept thinking of Cally. If a lottery win set friends dreaming, so would a crystal which could read minds. Actually, my crystal was far more amazing than any lottery win.

I'd told Cally too fast, hadn't I? I should have built up to it over weeks. No wonder her head was turned and she did something which just wasn't like her. Really I was as much to blame as Cally.

I remembered suddenly how the crystal had seemed to just slip out of my hand, and land right on top of that particular newspaper, that particular caption. Had Mrs Jameson meant me to see it? Was that her way of advising me?

For a moment I forgot to breathe, I was so excited. I was certain it wasn't just a coincidence. I was certain of something else, too. I had to sort things out with Cally right now.

Chapter Ten

The Only Way

I WENT ROUND to Cally's house straight after tea. I felt really nervous. I still wasn't sure what I was going to say to her.

Her mum answered the door. "Oh, hello, Matt," she said. I stepped inside the narrow hallway. Normally she'd have told me to go right upstairs. Today she just gave me this embarrassed smile.

"How's Cally?" I asked.

"Well, she's had this terrible migraine all day."

"Could I see her?"

Cally's mum looked even more embarrassed. "Actually, Matt, she said if you called she didn't want to see you . . ."

"Oh, OK." My voice fell away.

"Have you two had a falling-out?"

"Yes, we have, actually."

"Well, I wouldn't worry too much. I think she's very stressed at the moment." She lowered her voice. "Last night I caught her tearing this piece of paper up into smaller and smaller pieces."

Immediately I wondered if she'd been tearing up the test questions on *Julius Caesar.*

"And her father and I want her to do well at school, but not at the expense of her health. Above all, we want her to be happy."

"Sure."

The phone rang.

"Oh, will you excuse me, Matt. I'm sorry, I can't . . . but I'm sure . . . well, you and Cally have been friends for such a long time, haven't you? Do you mind seeing yourself out?"

She rushed away. I thought for a second, then sprinted upstairs. Cally and I shouldn't be hiding from each other. We should clear the air right now.

I knocked on Cally's door. No answer. I opened the door slowly.

"Hi, Cally, it's me. How are you doing?" I tried to sound bright and cheerful.

Still no answer.

Then I saw why: Cally was fast asleep. I was about to creep out again, when I remembered something.

With the aid of my crystal I can talk to people when they're asleep. They hear me, and I can overhear their thoughts.

I held the crystal and, after it had warmed up, said: "Cally, can you hear me?"

"Yes, I can hear you." Her voice sounded heavy with sleep. "But how . . . Is this a dream?"

"Yes, Cally, you could say that."

"Well, I want you to go away. How can I make you do that?" she hissed.

"Look, Cally, listen," I began.

"No, you listen. I'm so ashamed about what I did to you. I should never have written those notes. You're right, it was very nasty of me. I don't know what got into me. And now I just want to curl up and die."

"But, Cally, it was my fault too."

"No," she whispered, "don't try and be nice to me. I can't stand it. I let you down. The crystal will always come between us now . . . Please get out of my dream. Leave me alone."

The crystal was scorching hot so I had to let go of it. Cally's words ran around in my head, especially "The crystal will always come between us".

It was that sentence which decided me. I knew what I had to do next.

Once, when my sister Alison was

asleep I'd used the crystal to hypnotize her. It was the only way to get her to forget about the crystal's powers. It had been for the best. Now I had to hypnotize Cally. I didn't want to. But I had no choice.

I picked up the crystal. It had cooled down enough. I said, "Cally, it's me again."

She groaned.

"I'm going to help you, both of us. Just repeat after me . . ."

Suddenly, I heard footsteps on the stairs. I had to act fast.

"Repeat after me: 'Sunday night never happened. It's gone from my memory.'"

"Sunday night never happened. It's gone from my memory," she repeated.

"And the crystal . . ." But I couldn't

say any more because Cally's mum was in the doorway, staring at me in bewilderment.

"Matthew, I told you . . ."

"I know, I'm sorry, but I thought I could talk her round – only she's asleep."

Then Cally muttered, "And the crystal."

Cally's mum leant forward. "What's that, love?"

"And the crystal," she muttered again.

Cally's mum just shook her head. "Poor girl, she's got herself so wound up. I think it's best you leave now, Matthew."

"Yes, sure. Sorry."

I ran down those stairs. If only I'd been able to have a few moments longer with Cally.

Now I didn't know if I'd wiped the crystal from Cally's mind or not.

Chapter Eleven

A Terrible Shock

NEXT DAY CALLY was still away from school. I wondered if I should go and see her again. But when I got home my mum was waiting for me, smiling. She'd arranged for me to choose a dog from the Animal Rescue Centre.

I was really excited. Dad was still

away, but Alison came with Mum and me. The dog was to be my responsibility. I could pick the one I wanted, only not a big dog.

The dogs were in pens and as soon as they saw us they started barking madly.

"How do you stand the noise?" Mum asked the assistant who was showing us round.

"What noise?" replied the assistant.

As we walked by the dogs they ran to the front of their pens, showing themselves off. All except one. A brown and white spaniel who hid in the corner of his pen.

The assistant pointed at the spaniel. "Poor Scampi, he was in such a bad way when he came in here, all his hair had gone."

"Oh, that's terrible," I cried.

"And he'd been so badly neglected he had to go on a special diet because his stomach had shrunk."

No wonder the dog looked so sad.

"He's very affectionate to us," said the assistant, "but he's still very shy, so he keeps getting overlooked."

"I think he might take quite a bit of looking after," said Mum, half-pulling me away. She was pointing at a terrier who was jumping about and wagging his tail furiously. "Now, he looks ideal," she said.

But my eyes kept going back to Scampi.

Suddenly I grabbed the crystal. I can't pick up a dog's thoughts from it, but dogs can pick up mine. I tilted it towards Scampi and thought: "Scampi, you're a good dog, aren't you? And do you want to come back with me?"

Scampi's ears pricked up. I knew he could hear me.

"Scampi, if you want to come away with me, go over to the front of the pen now. Come on, boy, hurry up."

The next moment Scampi was pressing his nose right through the front of the pen. I went over to him. He looked up at me, then licked one of my fingers.

I knew he was the dog I had to have. Mum sighed a lot but agreed. We had a special chat with the assistant, who said she would visit us soon to see how Scampi was settling down.

Scampi slept on my lap all the way home. "He seems to have taken to you, anyhow," said Mum.

When we got home Mum let Scampi

have a wander around downstairs. Then he just ran round and round the garden as if he couldn't believe his luck; he was somewhere decent at last.

Mum gave me a long lecture on how I was taking on special responsibilities with Scampi. He still had an infection in his eyes and needed eye drops twice a day. It was up to me to remember, not Mum. She also said how Scampi was never to be allowed upstairs.

"Couldn't he just put two paws in my bedroom?" I asked.

"If I see him upstairs, he goes back right away," said Mum. "He sleeps in the utility room, not on your bed." She made up a basket for Scampi, and said if he cried in the night, on no account was I to go downstairs to him, otherwise we'd never get any peace.

I wasn't asleep long when his whining woke me up. I crept out on to the landing. A floorboard creaked and Mum called out: "No, Matt, I told you, leave him."

But it was hard to leave him, especially as he sounded so unhappy.

Then I decided to try something. I stole out on to the landing again, held my crystal tightly and thought: "Scampi, can you hear me, can you?"

Scampi gave a kind of yelp in reply.

"Good boy, now listen. Don't cry, you're in your new home – and everything's going to be great now."

I went on like this for ages. Scampi's cries gradually became fainter, then they stopped altogether.

Next morning my mum congratulated me. "Well done, Matt, for not going downstairs to Scampi. I told you he'd soon settle down, didn't I?"

I smiled to myself.

The doorbell rang. I opened the door. To my great surprise it was Cally.

"Well, don't look so shocked. I've only been away a couple of days," said Cally. "And thanks for not coming round to see me," she added sarcastically. "That's why I've come to call for you. Are you all right?"

"I'm fine," I spluttered.

Then Scampi appeared behind my legs. Of course Cally loved Scampi instantly, and we were both playing with him until Mum shooed us off to school.

We walked along together, chatting about Scampi. Cally seemed very cheerful, her old self again. So had my plan worked? Had she forgotten all about the crystal?

"One good thing about being away," she said, "I missed the *Julius Caesar* test. Were the questions hard?"

I drew a deep breath. "Yeah, a real Mrs Stacey special. I could only do two of them."

"I bet I couldn't have done any of them. I always seem to revise the wrong things. Still, last night I had this long chat with my mum and dad, and they said as long as I try, that's all they ask. They were really nice about it, actually."

So far, so good. I was tempted to use my crystal just to check Cally had really forgotten all about its powers. But in the end I didn't. I'd promised not to use the crystal on Cally. And from now on I was sticking to that vow.

Then I noticed something. It gave me a jolt. Cally wasn't wearing the ring I'd given her to mark us going out together.

"Where's your ring gone?" I asked.

She grinned. "I was laughing about that ring with my mum this morning. I can't imagine why I've had that on my finger for the past few days. Mum thinks it's because I was over-stressed."

I stopped dead. "But I gave you that ring."

"Oh, very funny. I remember where it came from all right: out of a cracker at my cousin's party."

"But you gave me the ring to give to you because . . ."

She leant across and felt my forehead. "Matt, what are you gabbling about?

That ring is nothing to do with you. How could it be?"

She was smiling, but looking puzzled as well.

With mounting horror I realized what I'd done. I'd removed the crystal from her memory all right, but I'd wiped out everything else from that evening too: including us going out together.

I walked around school in a daze all day. How could I have made Cally forget something so important as us going out together? I'd just have to ask her out again.

After school Cally came back to my house. Mum had stocked up with doggy things, including a collar and lead for Scampi. We took Scampi for a walk, then introduced him to Cally's dog, Bess. She sniffed this new impostor suspiciously at first, but soon the two dogs were tearing around the garden together.

And there were celebrations at Cally's house too. Her dad had just rung through to say he hadn't been selected for redundancy. Cally's mum said she'd been going out of her mind waiting.

Then she took me aside and said: "I'm really pleased you and Cally have sorted yourselves out."

But we hadn't sorted ourselves out. That was the problem.

So later, when Cally and I were sitting in the garden, watching the two dogs playing together, I asked her out again.

She turned me down flat. She said:

"I've been dreading you asking me that. I do like you. Of course I do. But if we went out together, and it didn't work out . . . well, we'd have nothing. And I'd have lost my best mate. So I don't think I could ever take that chance."

I wanted to say to her: "But you did take that chance – just a few nights ago." But of course she didn't remember anything about that now. That moment was lost for ever.

Maybe she'd only agreed to go out with me on Sunday because I had a magic crystal.

I'd never know now.

That was the problem with the crystal. It mixed up everything, poisoned everything.

I was supposed to stay at Cally's for

my tea. But I said I felt a bit sick and would go home. Instead, I took Scampi for another walk. We ended up going further than I'd intended: right on to the outskirts of the town. Scampi was enjoying himself anyway, sniffing everything appreciatively.

But I felt as if I'd been punched in the stomach. I took the crystal off my belt. I stared into it, watching all the different colours twisting and curling like a nest of snakes.

"You ruined Mrs Jameson's life," I muttered. "And now you're ruining mine. What do I want to look into people's heads for anyway? It only makes you lose all your friends. You've brought so many bad vibes into my life, I reckon my life would be much better without you."

I threw my hand holding the crystal right back. I really meant to chuck it in the bin opposite me, you know.

And I probably would have done if a voice hadn't whispered right in my ear: "What am I going to do? Someone help me, please."

Chapter Twelve

Merlin to the Rescue

I FROZE. WHAT had the crystal picked up now? It would only mean more trouble. But it was as if I'd received a distress signal. I couldn't ignore it, especially as the voice had sounded so young.

The crystal was pointing towards a

back street I'd never noticed before. "Come on, Scampi," I said. "We'll have a quick look, then we'll go home."

A second-hand shop took up the whole street. Sprawled down one side were ancient armchairs, sofas and cabinets; opposite, in front of a huge garage, loomed a small army of clapped-out fridges and cookers.

A man lurked in the shop doorway. He was a large, sweaty-looking man with tiny eyes. Scampi gave a low growl.

"Tie your dog up before you come in here."

"Shan't bother," I replied.

It certainly wasn't him the crystal had "overheard". Scampi and I wandered on down the street. The man stood watching us for a bit, then he went back inside his shop.

No one else seemed to be about. Yet the crystal had definitely "overheard" someone. I held it in front of me as if it were a metal detector searching out buried treasure.

The crystal quickly found that voice again. This is what I overheard: "Mum said, get out of my sight, William, I never want to see you again. And she won't. But what am I going to do? I can't stay here." Yet the voice still seemed to be coming out of thin air.

We were at the end of the street now. All that faced us was a large brown wardrobe. Scampi gave another growl. "Do you hear someone too?" I whispered.

Suddenly I opened the wardrobe door. And there, shrinking at the back, was a small boy who couldn't have been more than five or six.

I stared at him.

He stared back at me.

"Any particular reason why you're sitting in that wardrobe?" I asked.

"Just leave me alone," hissed the boy.

"What's your name?" I asked.

"Can't tell you that."

"It wouldn't be William, would it?"

The boy jumped in amazement. "But how did you know that?"

"Oh, I know lots of things – like, you've run away from home, haven't you?"

"Yes," squeaked the boy. Then he added: "You're magic, aren't you?"

I grinned. "Just call me Merlin."

But the boy took me seriously. "You're not Merlin the magician?"

"That's right. Only I'm in disguise, so don't tell anyone."

"I won't," gasped the boy.

"Now, I command you to climb out of that wardrobe."

The boy obeyed me instantly. He was shaking a bit. I think he was worried I was about to turn him into a toad.

"Why don't you give Scampi a pat?" I said.

The boy knelt down and gently, cautiously, patted Scampi.

"Tell me, what are you doing here?" I asked the boy.

"Don't you know?" he demanded.

"Of course I do. But I want you to tell me."

"All right, Merlin. Well, you know I broke my mum's special vase. And I really didn't mean to do it, but now she hates me. She said I'm nothing but trouble and she's sick of me. She told me to get out of her sight. And so I did.

"She thinks I'm in my room, but I crept out of the house and this bus pulled up, and I got on it. I sat with this woman and two other boys. They asked for a half-fare to Jericho Road, and so did I. I used up all my money too.

"I got off with them, but they weren't very friendly. Then the woman said she was going to take me to the police station, but I ran and ran, and I've got to hide here . . . for ever."

"You can't do that, William. You'll have to go back," I said.

"I can't," he cried.

"I'm commanding you," I said.

"Oh." He looked up. "Will you magic us back?"

"No, we'll get the bus this time," I said. "I only use magic for special occasions these days."

The three of us caught the bus back to William's home in Clately. It was nearly seven miles away, and the fare used up all the money I had saved for Cally's birthday. William sat cuddling Scampi. He noticed my crystal and wanted to hold it.

"Maybe, later," I said.

Then the bus drew into William's road. Suddenly he pointed. There was a woman talking animatedly into a mobile phone.

"That's my mum," he cried, "and she's going to be so mad at me."

"No she won't," I said.

"Yes she will. She looks really angry." The bus jolted to a stop. William hissed:

"I'm sorry, Merlin, but I can't get off this bus. Not even if you command me."

I thought quickly. "All right, William, I'm going to put a spell on you."

"Oooh." William looked both scared and excited.

"Here, hold my crystal."

He took the crystal.

Then I muttered (hoping no one else could hear me),

"Hocus Mucus, the magic spell will dawn
When this crystal starts to get warm."

A few seconds later William exclaimed: "It is getting hot, Merlin."

"Good, the spell is working. Move the crystal towards the window, and your mum."

"I don't want her to see me," said William, crouching down.

"Now, my magic spell is this: whatever your mum thinks will pour into your ear."

William looked at me, then let out a cry. "It's my mum talking right in my ear like you said. Can she hear me?"

I shook my head.

"She's saying, if anything's happened to William I'll never forgive myself. Never. All that fuss over a stupid vase. Now she's saying . . ."

The bus started to lurch forward. William looked at me, then screeched: "Make the bus stop, Merlin."

"Only you can do that," I said.

With that, William let out a great yell of "Stop" and the three of us scrambled off, just in time.

William's mum spotted William and came flying towards us at a speed any Olympic athlete would have envied. She and William hugged and kissed each other while Scampi and I felt a bit awkward.

But then William's mum insisted Scampi and I come inside for tea and cakes. We also met just about every one of the neighbours who'd all been out looking for William.

Then William's dad arrived – he'd rushed home from work. And later he insisted on driving us home (just as well, as I only had ten pence left) and telling my startled mum just what I'd done.

After he'd left, Mum said: "I'm really proud of you. If you hadn't discovered that boy goodness knows what would have happened to him . . . You know, you might even have saved his life."

Then she added: "Just one thing, why did William's dad keep calling you Merlin?"

"Oh, it's a long story, Mum," I said, and quickly changed the subject. Knowing I'd helped William gave me a good feeling. Of course it was the crystal, really. How could I ever have thought of chucking it away? That would have been so stupid – and cowardly.

Mrs Jameson must have realized I'd make some mistakes with the crystal. But she'd believed in me too. And one day I know I'll become the crystal master. Then, when I'm very old and have to decide who to pass the crystal on to next, I'll write down everything I've learnt. A kind of guide book.

Rule one will be: never use the crystal on your family, your mates – or your girlfriend.

No, Cally isn't my girlfriend yet. But I haven't given up hope. She did agree to go out with me once. It's just a shame she doesn't remember anything about it now. Still, I know she thinks I'm fit. And I can bask in that.

Whatever happens with Cally in the future, the crystal stays out of it. I'm only using my crystal on one friend at the moment. Can you guess who?

Well, I'll tell you. Every afternoon after I leave Cally I pick up my crystal and start beaming thoughts to Scampi. His hearing, by the way, is amazing. He can pick up from over a mile away.

I say to him: "Come on, Scampi,

come and meet me. Go to the door, there's a good boy."

At once he starts scratching at the front door, whining to be let out. Then he charges off and sits right outside the gate just as I'm about to turn into my road.

My neighbours think it's uncanny how he always knows exactly when I'm coming home. So, if I'm late because of football practice, Scampi will just ask to be let out later too.

He never gets it wrong.

Half of my road come out to observe this amazing phenomenon now. "It's magic to watch," one of them said yesterday.

Thanks to the crystal my life is full of magic. Just about anything could happen. Maybe one day I'll even pick up your thoughts. Wouldn't that be great?

I'll be listening.